D1084196

About the Book

Sundance and four other coyote cubs were born to a harsh life. The once-lush prairie had long since become a semiarid scrubland, and many animals, including the buffalo, were extinct. Some animals, such as the kangaroo rat, had adapted physically to the changed environment. The coyote, already possessed of great speed and stamina, had to adapt by *learning* to survive.

The innately alert, wary temperament of the cubs, the care and experiences gained from their parents, and the prowess developed through exploration and play enable some to survive. Branded a "killer" by the white man, the coyote must be suspicious of any sign of change in his range. Food may be poisoned; new lures are continually being invented; hunters in jeeps are often on the prowl with their dogs. Sandboy, Sylvia, and other cubs who are headstrong and curious do not adapt to the threat of human predation and are often killed. When the cubs are ten months old, they must find their own range in the ever-decreasing space available. Sundance's range is near an Indian reservation.

The coyote has long been sacred to the Indian, and fortunately a kinship develops between Sundance and the chief's son, Laughing Dog. Life seems easier for Sundance, but an ingrained coyote trait causes him to be trapped.

Dr. Fox again shows his unique ability to describe animals' communication and their relationships with each other and the environment. Focusing on the activities of Sundance and his family, Dr. Fox shows how all life on the semiarid scrubland is interrelated.

This clear discussion not only helps us understand the much-maligned coyote, but also contributes to our respect for the basic laws of nature, making us more aware of our own responsibilities and commitment to the preservation of wildlife. Dee Richmann researched her accurate illustrations by observing and sketching Dr. Fox's own coyotes.

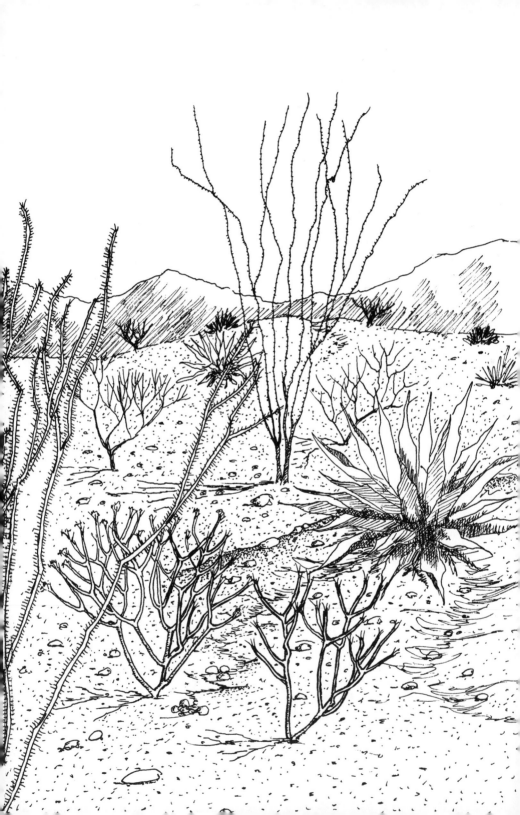

SUNDANCE COYOTE

by Dr. Michael Fox

ILLUSTRATED BY DEE GATES

Coward, McCann & Geoghegan, Inc.
New York

Contents

For children and other sundancers

Preface

This is a story about a Western coyote named Sundance who lives in the semidesert rangeland typical of eastern New Mexico and northwest Texas. It tells of his life and of the dangers, hardships and joys in this arid scrubland that was once lush prairie.

The behavior and mind of the coyote is described in order to give a clear and sensitive image of this much-maligned "varmint." Sundance and his kind are not misfits but are an integral part of the balance and harmony in all of nature. In man's world where the coyote does not fit to man's satisfaction, he is outlawed and persecuted. If man is to save himself, he must help conserve the sense of the earth and be in balance with the natural world. This involves an appreciation for and understanding of the lives and rights of others—fellow human beings and animals alike.

The story of Sundance and of his bond with the Indian boy, Laughing Dog, is for our children, to help foster in them a sense of the earth and to give them a feeling for the lives of others on this earth that we must keep green, bright and beautiful.

I

The Death of
the Prairie

Sundance came from a long line of
prairie coyotes, but none of his family for eight or ten
generations before him had known the prairie as it once
was. Coyotes live for six to eight years, although over
half die in their first year of life. It was more than eighty
years since the first pioneer settlers had moved onto the
prairie and begun its destruction.

In the days before the settlers arrived, rolling miles of
long, green grass seemed like a vast green ocean when the
prairie winds moved over it. Many kinds of grasses,
teeming with seed-eating insects and mice, grew from

the rich soil. The prairie provided food for other vegetarians too. Prairie dogs lived in community villages or
coteries, numbering in the millions over thousands of
acres of land. Prairie chickens, ground squirrels,

gophers, rabbits and badgers thrived. Meadowlarks and longspurs flew on the wind and rose into the blue sky, singing above great herds of buffalo and pronghorn antelopes. These herds grazed and moved on, never

staying too long in one place, thus preventing the prairie from being damaged by overgrazing.

These vegetarians were part of the natural food chain for the flesh-eating animals or predators that roamed the prairie. If the surplus population of the plant-eating animals that were too small to migrate with the buffalo and the antelope were not controlled by predators, they might have eventually killed the prairie by overgrazing.

The predators that kept this natural balance were many. Various kinds of hawks and eagles plummeted from the sky to grab the unwary in ironlike talons. Packs of wolves followed the herds removing the old, the sick and the unhealthy young. And Indians on swift ponies also took their share of big game. Like the wolf, they never killed too many, or there would have been no food for tomorrow.

Smaller predators—shrews with poisonous saliva, badgers, skunks and black-footed ferrets—prayed on insects, grubs, worms and rodents, such as mice and voles.

Coyotes also hunted these smaller animals, as well as cleaning up the remains left by wolves. They also ate dead animals or carrion, but their main source of food was the swift jackrabbit. Coyotes are built with the long legs and deep chests, the speed and agility, to catch these elusive rabbits. A coyote can turn on a dime at full speed (up to forty miles per hour) and grab a racing, zigzagging jackrabbit.

The prairie was a rich world, the good earth support-ing many different kinds of animals, from vegetarians large and small, such as mice and bison, to predators such as the wolf, Indian and coyote. All lived together in balance until the white settlers came.

The land rush began a little less than a hundred years ago. Pioneers realized that the rich prairie was good grazing land for their stock, and when plowed, it was ideal for raising grains. Domesticated animals and plants—sheep and cattle and wheat and corn—rapidly replaced all that was prairie. The wild perennial prairie grasses were plowed under and billions of golden bushels of grain were harvested. Cattle and sheep grazed and fattened where once the buffalo and pronghorn antelope roamed.

But all too soon, "wars" erupted between sheepmen and cattlemen. Although both cattle and sheep grazed, the sheep were more destructive to the grasses than the cattle because they nibbled everything down to the roots. The cattlemen were justly afraid that the sheep would turn the prairie into a desert, as they have done in Spain and North Africa. But the cattle were also destructive, and soon the original wild animals of the prairie faded away, as the prairie grasses on which they depended were destroyed. With no cover for nesting, quail, for example, once almost as numerous as the prairie dog, became scarce. But hunters placed the blame on the coyote.

Man was also directly responsible for the destruction of wildlife on the prairie. Because the prairie dogs ate the grasses that the ranchers wanted for their stock, they began to destroy the prairie-dog towns with poison. Many animals, including coyotes, badgers, wildcats and foxes, relied heavily on the prairie dog as part of their diet. When the prairie dogs were destroyed and the food chain broken, many of these predators died of starvation. A few large ones, such as the coyotes and wildcats, were able to hold on, but they had to turn to sheep for food. Coyotes were branded as killers when they killed calves or sheep, but they, like the Indians, had little else to eat. They became renegades with a bounty on their heads. Local trappers and later government officials with deadly poisons joined the fight against the coyote, killing other innocent animals, too—badgers, skunks, rabbits and birds.

A few wise cattle farmers saw the coyote as an ally who kept down the jackrabbits that ate the grass almost as greedily as his own stock. But most farmers, and especially the sheep farmers, saw all wildlife as a threat and continued their war against nature—poisoning, shooting and trapping everything. In their ignorance, they were killing the prairie that was their livelihood. Their greed for more made them destroy the source of their riches.

Almost overnight the prairie changed. The buffalo and the antelope were shot for sport and because they competed for the same food as the farmer's cattle and sheep; they were soon nearly extinct. Indians, whose lives depended on the buffalo, had nothing left to hunt. They and the wolves dwindled and starved.

With the destruction of the prairie grasses, less nutritious and palatable weeds as well as inedible sagebrush and mesquite took their place. Since the poison baits had killed off the predators that had kept down the grass-eating rodents and grasshoppers, they began to flourish and together with the cattle soon completely destroyed the prairie. Accidental fires that were essential for the normal growth of the prairie were put out by farmers who did not understand and who already were becoming worried over the tired and worn state of the grazing land. With the prairie grasses dying and the sod or turf topsoil becoming hard and impervious through trampling and summer drought, the precious rains of spring were not absorbed. The water ran off the land into gullies and was wasted. Then the winds came, and where the sod had been broken by the plow there were no prairie-grass roots to hold the rich topsoil and so it was blown away. The prairie died and became a desert.

The elusive, strong and wily coyote was one of the few members of the prairie world to hold on. No matter how the settlers tried to destroy them with snares, steel traps and poisoned baits, some still survived. The more the hunters tried, the cleverer the coyote became in evading them. Hundreds of thousands of coyotes died, but those that survived were the most intelligent. From this noble heritage came Sundance.

From the very beginning, life was to be a long fight for the little coyote. A fight against man and a fight for survival in all that remained of the prairie—a semiarid desert of sagebrush and dust. Sundance would have to learn how to live in this worst of all possible worlds.

2

The Sun Rises

Sundance was born in a den hidden between two large rocks that ages before had fallen to form an upside-down V. Moonshadow, his mother, had enlarged the little cave by digging several feet into the ground. Before she moved in, other animals had lived there. Most recently, she knew by the smell, there had been a skunk, and before that a badger, judging from the litter of bones and stuff. In a crevice in the cave some seeds, a button, a few bright pebbles and a used shotgun cartridge had been carefully stored by an avid collector of novelties—the pack rat.

The den, well hidden by willows and cottonwood, was on the side of a rain-washed gully or arroyo that carried the spring rains in flash floods. On the far side lay miles of scrub—sagebrush, mesquite, yucca, agave, prickly pear and bunchgrass. This was once prairie land, but now only a few range cattle could be seen during the day and the occasional scorpion, buzzard and desert cottontail rabbit. Gone were the prairie-dog villages, the prairie chickens and most of the plump jackrabbits—all staple food for the coyote. Gone, too, were the buffalo, peccaries or wild pigs, and pronghorn antelopes. By day, the scrubland looked like a bleak wilderness, a barren land upon which to raise a family of coyotes.

There were four other dark brown bodies in the den along with Sundance, and their parents worked day and night to bring them enough food. Although it was springtime, little rain had fallen so that the usual lush spring vegetation was reduced. Because of this, there was not enough green food for mice and rabbits and their young. Since these little animals were the staple diet of the coyotes, the coyotes suffered indirectly from the poor spring growth of plants. Sundance's parents ranged far in search of food, their urgency increasing when his mother's milk supply began to dry up and the cubs were five weeks old and ready for weaning onto solid food.

At night the half-desert scrubland was more alive than during the day. Nocturnal animals came out after resting in the daytime to avoid the heat. This way they would not get so thirsty. Soon after sunset, Moonshadow and Longface, her mate, would howl together and then set out, first up the dry river bed to a muddy water hole.

Here they would stalk and sometimes catch a thirsty animal. After a quick drink themselves, they would scour the scrubland for mice, kangaroo rats, and insects. They would swallow anything edible and carry it home in their stomachs to be regurgitated for their young. Usually one of them would return earlier than the other to guard over the cubs, although they could ill afford to do this, since two can hunt better than one. Many times Longface would return with a little food and Moonshadow would set out at dawn to try her luck. At dawn, the nocturnal animals were going back into their holes and the crepuscular animals—those active at dusk and dawn but who rested most of the day and night—were out.

Sometimes Longface and Moonshadow would bring home a scrawny rock squirrel, a garter snake and a handful of grasshoppers, or two or three deer mice, and a spiny or collared lizard or a larger chuckwalla lizard if they were lucky. On rare occasions they might catch a few birds, a sage grouse, or a quail.

Bobcats, vultures and red-tailed hawks competed with them for these sources of food. By scavenging and hunting most of the time, each taking turns to rest and to guard the cubs, the devoted parents were able to raise all five of them through the difficult weaning period. Both parents were scrawny, their coats dry and broken, but their cubs were strong and healthy.

On the near or east side of the gully where their den was located, the scrubland sloped upward after a few miles, the bunchgrass and sagebrush giving way to piñon and juniper trees and scattered agaves, yuccas and prickly-pear cacti. Piñon nuts, mesquite beans and juniper berries were staple food for many animals and this higher land was richer than the semidesert scrubland that Moonshadow and Longface occupied. They could not move into this more hospitable land because it was already held by other families of coyotes.

Moonshadow could enter one of the neighbor's territories since her brother had his stake there. His mate, however, was very aggressive toward visitors, and so it was more usual for Moonshadow's brother to visit her, since Longface was usually a friendly animal.

Coyotes obey the strict rules of territoriality or property rights. They do not trespass on each other's hunting range. If there were no such pattern and those with no food robbed from those whose land could barely support them alone, they would all soon starve. When food is scarce, coyotes are more aggressive toward strangers entering their territory, but when there is abundance of food they may be more friendly and sociable, at least for a while.

Coyotes are not only fitted physically to their environments, having great speed, stamina and heat resistance; they also adapted socially and emotionally to their environment. The challenge of the desert is perhaps one of the greatest of all. Other animals have adapted physically even better. Some, like the kangaroo rat and pocket mouse need no water—they can live off dry seeds alone and come out only at night, preferring to stay in their burrows during the day to avoid the sun. Desert lizards, snakes and many insects do not pass any water. They absorb everything and pass out dry uric acid. Countless insects, such as desert plants, have a waxy, waterproof covering that stops water from evaporating in the heat. In cold regions, many warm-blooded animals hibernate to avoid the winter. Likewise in the desert, some avoid the heat by becoming sleepy and aestivating. When in these states, their bodies need little or no food or water.

Most desert plants protect themselves from animals with thorns and spines; some remain dormant and avoid the dry periods, only flowering after a brief rain. They produce millions of seeds because only a few will survive and take root. Certain shrubs produce a chemical substance that stops other plants from growing near them. Like coyotes, they need territorial space for their roots to grow and collect water and nutrients from the earth, so they have developed a means to keep away from each other.

Many desert plants and animals are already adapted to the desert—they are made that way and know what to do. But for Sundance it was different. He would have much to learn if he was to survive, and he not only had the hardships of the scrubland to contend with, but also man, on whose land and "legal" territory he and his family were trespassing.

3

Survival School

Although the coyote cubs had well-developed, needle-sharp canine teeth at two weeks of age, they were not ready to take solid food until a week later. Even so, growls and yelps echoing from the dark insides of the den were evidence that the cubs were doing more with their teeth than just eating what their parents gave them.

Coyote cubs between three and five weeks of age are always getting into fights, and Sundance and his brother and sisters were no exception. Just imagine a scrawny, pot-bellied, short-sighted, wobbly bundle of energy that pokes its nose into everything and grabs and bites anything furry whenever it gets excited. That's a coyote cub!

By six weeks or so they have usually learned to bite gently when they play, so fights are rare. Their teeth are so sharp that it is amazing that little serious harm is done during those first encounters with each other. As it was, one of Sundance's sisters had a drooping ear which had been damaged by Sandboy, who was the biggest cub of the litter. And Sundance had a limp for a few days after a serious fight with Sandboy.

The fight had started when the cubs were sleeping in the den. Droopy, the female with the bad ear and her sisters, Sylvia and Celeste, were piled on top of Sundance and Sandboy. Suddenly Celeste started whimpering in her sleep and making running movements with her stubby little legs. She was having a bad dream. This startled Sundance who was just daydreaming, and he struggled out from under the sweet-hay-smelling mound of cubs and woke everyone up. One by one they stretched, yawned, and except for Sylvia and Droopy, who were exhausted from an afternoon of chasing grasshoppers, wobbled to the cool entrance of the den. The evening air quickly brought them to life. Celeste started to play with a piece of rabbit skin, first bowing low, then twisting her hips to one side and then to the other. This was the beginning of an instinctual coyote dance which consists of bowing, twisting from side to side, spinning around and even diving and rolling. Some old-timers reckon that a coyote will do this to fascinate or lure and

trap a rabbit or a duck. The curious animals will stand and stare or even approach until the coyote is close enough to grab it. More than one person claims to have seen a coyote dance under a tree and mesmerize roosting turkeys until one of the dizzy birds falls off its perch.

Suddenly Celeste lost her balance and rolled over and was stuck there for several seconds like a turtle on its back. As she tried to get up, one of her legs touched Sundance in the groin. Now when a young coyote is touched here, he stays quite still. Sometimes he might accidentally brush against a twig or a knobby root and will remain still for several seconds if his side or groin is touched. They grow out of this, and adult coyotes will touch groins as a friendly gesture—like people shaking hands. One coyote will twist its flank toward its fellow and remain quite still when its companion touches it lightly in the groin with its nose.

Sundance froze when Celeste touched him, and Sandboy, seeing Sundance standing over Celeste, thought that they were having a fight. He ran over to them and put both forepaws stiffly on top of Sundance's shoulders. Sundance growled at Sandboy. Celeste, thinking that Sundance was going to fight with her, screamed and gave him a frightened nip on the elbow. Thoroughly confused, Sundance tried to get away from Celeste, but to move when someone is standing over you is a challenge. So as soon as he moved, Sandboy grabbed him by the shoulder and, shaking his head violently from side to side, drove his long, sharp teeth deep into Sundance. Sundance twisted away at once but could not break Sandboy's viselike hold. The two fighting cubs rolled over and over, Sandboy holding on and Sundance twisting and snapping. Celeste ran back into the den, leaving the two male cubs to settle their differences once and for all. As soon as cubs learn which of their companions are weaker or stronger, they no longer fight seriously, but the only way they learn is through fighting. This was the dominance fight for Sundance and Sandboy. Sandboy was bigger and had the advantage of size and weight, but Sundance was fast and more coordinated.

Sandboy lost his hold on Sundance, and this gave Sundance the chance to grab Sandboy's cheek. Since Sandboy was stronger, he was able to twist around and bite Sundance several times on the shoulder and forefeet. This was too much for Sundance. He let go of Sandboy, pulled his lips back in a surrendering grin of submission, and yelping, rolled over onto his back and remained completely still. Instantly Sandboy stopped his attack and stood stiffly over Sundance with tail straight out, his mouth puckered into a snarl. Each knew the limits of the other and from now on they would respect each other. Neither had really lost. Sandboy would never bully Sundance or any of his sisters, but he would have first choice from now on of food and the most comfortable sleeping place.

When the others were eating or in possession of a bone or some plaything, Sandboy would obey the unwritten law that being owner of something meant that the owner had his way, even if he was a low-ranking coyote. What was his, was his, so long as he was in possession of it. Sandboy would never browbeat any of the others into surrendering what they had.

From this time on, since each cub knew where it stood, life was more peaceful. The days and nights were filled less with growls and yelps and more with the silence that meant coordinated and cooperative actions related to the serious business of exploring their world; what to eat, where to find it, and how to catch and kill it. Longface and Moonshadow often helped their cubs' schooling by bringing back injured prey for them to chase, catch and kill.

While one or both parents were away hunting, the cubs busied themselves among the rocks and bushes along the arroyo, sometimes even venturing across the gully into the open scrubland beyond. The farther away they got from the den, the more nervous they were at the slightest strange noise or sudden movement. Celeste, who was the most timid, usually ran straight back to the den, while Sundance and Droopy, who were both cautious cubs, would either freeze or run to the nearest bush or rock pile and then poke their heads out curiously seconds later. Sandboy and Sylvia were the most outgoing and tended to go off together. Celeste usually tagged behind Sundance and Droopy, who also spent much of their time together.

Grasshoppers singing in the bushes and lizards sunning in the early morning before the stones became too hot, were favorite sport. They rarely caught lizards, but grasshoppers provided a juicy reward for little work. The cubs had keen ears that helped them find exactly where a grasshopper was singing, and quick eyes that detected the slightest movement. At first the cubs were clumsy in their attempts to hunt for themselves. Sand-

27

boy always seemed top-heavy, and after a wild rush he would do a nose dive and go head over heels. Once, but never again, he did one of his spectacular dives into a thorn bush. The other cubs were watching him when it happened, and they learned to "look before you leap." Thorns hurt. Many insects and tasty, four-legged creatures sought safety in the thorny shrubs and cactus plants that covered the arid scrubland.

Aside from their stalking and ambush game, another favorite sport was like the game of moving statues or red light, green light—stop and go. You follow behind someone, stopping even in mid-stride when he turns around and looks at you. You lose if he sees you move, and you win if you get close enough to touch the person in front of you. The coyote cubs played this game for hours, often combining it with ambushing. Two would be playing moving statues and a third would stalk and ambush one of the others. The moving statues game they would soon learn to adopt when hunting rabbits and other game. Such animals are quick to notice anything that moves and are easily alarmed. But they settle down quickly and continue about their business when what was moving stops moving. It's as though they only see or recognize a coyote when it is moving. So a coyote creeps up, closer and closer, edges forward when the rabbit continues to feed, and freezes when the rabbit sees it moving and turns to look. An adult coyote can freeze in mid-stride, stay on three legs and not twitch a whisker or flick an ear for ages. Hunting is neither play or pleasure; it is serious business when food means survival.

Sundance was the first to discover a special, coyote hunting-action. Instead of stalking and then rushing and grabbing, he would stalk and then rear up, to come down with stiff forelegs right on top of a grasshopper, trapping it under his paws. A couple of stabs—short up and down jumps—would injure the insect, so that it could not get away before he grabbed it in his jaw. The other cubs developed this inborn action, since it was the best way to catch small prey—and better to have a thorn or two in the paw that's easily pulled out, than one in the nose! Their coordination and speed got better as they practiced on grasshoppers. This would be useful when they went after bigger and more difficult prey such as deer mice and rabbits.

When Sundance and Droopy were exploring together, they were the first to begin to realize the advantages of team hunting. One cub would walk ahead of the other, stirring up grasshoppers for its alert partner, who would grab them as soon as they landed nearby.

The cubs were learning to live off the land and to provide for themselves, picking up tips from their parents constantly. A few scrapes under a prickly-pear tree would expose succulent thirst-quenching roots, free from thorns. The tender sweet tunas, fruit of the prickly-pear cactus were also edible and only needed a few rubs and rolls against the ground with a paw to remove the fine thorns. Odorless mesquite beans that looked like worthless chips of rock were filling and quite nutritious.

4

Growing Up Together

When the cubs were six weeks old, Moonface and Longshadow started to take them to the water hole regularly at dusk. The cubs followed behind Moonshadow in single file, often stumbling and rolling over or breaking file to follow some curious smell with their inquisitive noses. Longface held up the rear, nudging stragglers with his moist muzzle and encouraging them to keep up with Moonshadow.

Their first experience at the water hole was a memorable event, since none of the cubs had ever seen water or drunk out of a pool before. The only fluids they had tasted were their mother's milk and water regurgitated for them by Longface and Moonshadow. Sandboy and Sylvia were first to reach the water. Sandboy growled at his reflection, and in pawing at it lost his balance and fell in. The splash frightened Celeste, who hid between Longface's feet. Sylvia and then Sundance, followed by Droopy, edged cautiously forward and, seeing Sandboy paddling and snapping at the water, were soon tumbling and chasing each other in the shallows, churning up the mud and splattering each other. In no time at all the four cubs looked like half-drowned rats with their hair plastered down over their skinny, leggy frames. Celeste didn't seem to recognize them and acted upset, but with a little urging from Longface she eventually joined the other "mud larks" in the pool, which by now was no more than a churned-up mud puddle.

A small, sheltered hollow above the arroyo served as a sunning place where the family could rest during the hot day. Here, Moonshadow lay in front of Longface and he gently and thoroughly groomed her, nibbling and pulling burrs, thorns and matted hair from her coat and affectionately licking her lips, eyelids and ears. Then she groomed him while one or more of the cubs stalked his tail, pouncing and pulling on it furiously. Moonshadow was more strict with the cubs and rarely allowed them to do this. A low growl and a quick stare from her was enough to make them instantly roll over onto their backs. When the parents had finished tending each other, they groomed the cubs and finally trekked back to the den, Longface heading off alone on an early night hunt.

Regular visits to the drinking hole now began with an excited group ceremony. Longface and Moonshadow would lick and nuzzle and nibble the pups fondly and begin squeaking and whining as though to rouse them for something important. This was a little like the way the cubs would greet their parents when they came back from hunting, but instead it was the parents who rallied around the cubs. The whole family would go off, all wagging their tails, licking their faces, nuzzling and bumping each other, the squeaking and whining noises sounding just like laughter.

By the time the cubs were four months old, they were regularly going off alone or in pairs to hunt and scavenge by themselves. In the evening they joined up at the hollow near the water hole—their favorite meeting place. These evening get-togethers were always accompanied by much excited greeting, followed by first one and then the other giving little yips and barks. These sounds were followed by a group "sing along." With heads pointing to the starry sky, the family engaged in the ancient coyote ritual of the evening chorus. It seemed as though there were a hundred coyotes in the hollow, their voices rising and falling, splitting into a shower of notes that bounced and echoed on the rocks. Some of the sounds were soft and melodious, others gay and joyous, rising in a wild crescendo and tumbling from crazy heights into giggly jumbles of yips and muffled barks. Longface could even throw his voice like a ventriloquist and make it come out of a nearby boulder or mesquite bush. When the family chorus was over, they could hear others in neighboring territories singing too. Longface and Moonshadow listened closely to the others' singing; perhaps they were saying something to each other.

We don't really know what the coyotes communicate to each other in their songs. It is said that some Indians who have met coyotes in their dreams know what some of their songs mean and they will tell no one else since they are bound to secrecy. Some think that coyotes sing more when there is going to be a change in the weather. Others, who hear coyotes often, only remember hearing them when something unusual happens, like an old man dying in the village. A legend grows saying that coyotes singing means someone has died.

The cubs were beginning to roam farther and farther from home and coming across all kinds of surprises. Early one evening, Sundance and Droopy were going over a pile of rocks, poking their noses into every nook and cranny, hoping to get a chance at a lizard or a rock squirrel. Sundance was about to leap up onto a flat rock

when a sudden rattling noise made him start and fall off the rock. It was a good thing he did fall, because that flat rock was the favorite sunning spot of an old rattlesnake.

The two coyotes carefully edged around the flat rock and looked at the deadly poisonous snake from a distance. The other cubs, Celeste, Sandboy and Sylvia, spotted the two cubs and seeing that they had found something exciting, ran over to have a look too. Sandboy, who was strong-headed, was likely to get bitten,

but before he and the others reached Sundance and Droopy, Longface joined them and gave the alarm signal—a low, growl-bark which meant "look out." Obediently the cubs kept back, learning at once that snakes were to be avoided.

Longface was an experienced snake hunter, and on his light, quick feet he edged toward the snake, which rattled a warning. Then he pretended to jump forward. The snake struck out at him, but he was out of reach. He kept this up for half an hour, lunging close to the snake, but just out of reach, and slowly he was tiring the snake. Suddenly, instead of pretending to bite at the snake, he actually leaped at it and with one swift bite behind the head, killed it instantly. The long body of the snake writhed and twisted for a while, and then Longface began to eat it. The cubs tried the meat too, but they did not like it.

The cubs were lucky that no one was bitten, since many a curious and unwary young coyote is killed by poisonous snakes. Longface had survived a bite from a rattler when he was young and had developed a taste for killing snakes.

Moonshadow joined the group around the snake. She clearly did not approve of Longface's killing the snake and possibly encouraging the cubs to attack snakes in the future. She cautiously sniffed the remains of the snake, urinated on it and then snapped at Longface and the cubs and drove them away from the deadly reptile. The cubs would know to avoid such snakes as the sidewinders, coral snakes and rattlers that abound in the scrublands.

5

To the Edge of Their World

Early next morning the family took off together, trotting up the hillside at the back of their den. Moonshadow and Longface were taking their children on a long tour to the far limits of their territory, up to the higher land where piñon and juniper trees flourished. They were moving toward the territory of Moonshadow's brother.

As they trotted along, piñon jays chattered and cursed at them, warning each other and many other animals around too, that someone dangerous was coming close. A tiny, golden-brown kit fox shot out from behind a rock right in front of Longface, and for a moment stood there cheekily staring with his big ears sticking right up and his bushy tail arched over his back. Sundance decided to chase the little desert fox, but with one whisk of his long fluffy tail, the fox went zig-zag-zzzig and disappeared like magic down a hole hardly as big as Sundance's head. This was his first meeting with a very distant cousin. Kit foxes were rare in the region now, since most had been killed by poison baits meant for coyotes. Unlike coyotes, they are not so cautious and are easily trapped and poisoned.

A little farther, the cubs came to a narrow valley, where they drank from a spring and then settled down to rest briefly in the shade of a large juniper bush. The cubs, imitating their parents, began to scrape up the earth to make cool scoop holes in which to lie. A jay, who made his home in this tree, was surprised to see the family of coyotes there, and suddenly began chattering and screaming at them. He was soon joined by three others and the coyotes decided that they would have little rest there, so they got up and set off across the valley. The jays chased them, swooping and diving while the cubs tried to catch the elusive birds. Celeste was afraid but she soon settled down after seeing how her parents ignored the mobbing of the birds.

By now it was late afternoon and the cubs were getting hungry. Before they turned back to begin the long journey home, the family came upon an old juniper stump that stood up like a landmark in an open stretch of

the hillside. Longface and Moonshadow circled it, sniffing intently. The cubs had seen their parents doing this before at other spots—sometimes a particular bush or protruding rock on the plains. This was one of the scent posts at the edge of their territory which they would mark with the scent of their urine. Neighboring coyotes would leave their mark, too. A coyote had passed by recently and since the scent was quite fresh, Longface was aroused. The hair along his back bristled and he marked the stump several times, finally scraping the earth around it with his feet to leave an additional mark. The cubs sniffed the post too, recognizing the familiar and fading scents of their parents from earlier visits to the marker, as well as the odors of two or three other coyotes that they had yet to meet. Two of these were Moonshadow's brother and his mate, the third was a stranger to both Moonshadow and Longface. This stranger was, in fact, an old male who had given up his territory after his mate had died. He had passed by in search of a new mate and left his mark long before the cubs were born.

Just around sunset the coyotes were making their way down a narrow ravine. The cubs were almost as big as their parents now, but their long, nimble legs did not have the same tireless jaunty spring as their parents'. Every now and then one of the cubs would trip or slip, or stop to investigate something and then go racing and stumbling anxiously back to the others as soon as they got out of sight. Once they stopped when Sundance, who was at the end of the line, caught the smell of something strange in a sudden breeze that cut across the ravine. The smell was sweet, heavy and very strong. It was close and the wind told him the direction. He cautiously jumped onto a rock for a better look and there on the other side, right beneath his feet, was a porcupine—unaware that a coyote was above him. Sundance realized that this animal was small enough to kill, but for one moment before he leaped on top of the animal, he hesitated. That moment saved his life. More than one young coyote has leaped onto a porcupine intending to bite it through the back, only to get mouth, face, paws and even eyes full of quills. The pain could drive them into a frenzy, and they would keep on attacking, injuring themselves more and more. They would be in pain for days, then numbness would come as the quill wounds became infected, and finally death.

At that last moment the porcupine saw Sundance out of the corner of one almost invisible beady black eye, and he instantly turned his back on the coyote, whipped his tail, raised his quills and rattled them. Some of the quills on the porcupine are hollow to make this display even more impressive. Sundance remembered the sound of the rattlesnake and in his alarm fell over backward off the rock. The other coyotes heard the porcupine, and in seconds the prickly old scavenger was surrounded by the seven of them. Each time one of the coyotes broke the circle and advanced or even showed the slightest intention of coming closer, the porcupine rattled his quills louder than ever. Moonshadow gave Sandboy the warning bark when he got too close. The coyotes kept their respectful distance for some time. Then the porcupine put his quills down and ambled off, walking right between Moonshadow and Longface, who didn't even flick an ear as he went by. The cubs knew to respect porcupine from then on.

Some people claim that a porcupine can actually shoot the quills out like missiles when it is being attacked, but there is no truth in this old wives' tale. Some coyotes however, like Longface who was an expert snake killer, can become efficient porcupine getters. They make the porcupine run, or wait until it walks away and with a quick sideways attack, flip it over onto its back. There

are no protective quills on the animal's underside and it is easy and safe then for the coyote to kill it.

The porcupine that Sundance discovered had been picking at the remains of a dead skunk, but there was little left for the coyotes to eat. The cubs investigated it carefully but did not touch it. They knew that the bright black and white colors of the skunk might mean danger. Many animals, instead of having camouflaging colors and patterns to conceal them, have bright colors that serve as

a warning to others. Poisonous creatures such as coral snakes, some salamanders and insects such as hornets have these colors. The skunk's markings, plus the overpowering scent that he can shoot out at an enemy, make up his defense, since he has no other weapons like the porcupine's quills or the armor plate of a hard shell like the desert armadillo or tortoise to keep off larger animals.

After investigating the skunk himself, Longface rolled in the smelly remains with an expression of obvious pleasure on his face. Coyotes, like dogs and wolves, find much enjoyment in rolling in all kinds of odoriferous things. Wearing a strong scent for them is perhaps like a human being putting on a brightly-colored shirt or blouse that gives us visual pleasure, as well as drawing the attention of others.

As Longface made his last, ecstatic diving roll onto the dead animal, he kicked over a small rock with one of his legs. This was the home of a golden female scorpion. She had a brood of young ones and was alarmed when she suddenly felt her safe refuge was gone. Immediately she arched her tail over her back, on the end of which was her sting. She was ready to strike and rushed at Longface who was only inches away. He was completely unaware of what had happened. Moonshadow, whose quick eyes never missed anything that moved, reached the scorpion in one leap and with a lightning, Karate-like stab with a foreleg, crushed the insect. Her speed was not enough to avoid the scorpion's strike, and at the moment she struck, she herself was stung. Whether she did this to stop her mate from being stung, or whether she was reacting to the movement of the creature and her own intense dislike for scorpions, only she knew. Fortunately this kind of scorpion was not very poisonous—some are deadly. Before the fire of its poison spread into her leg, she had eaten the insect, but not before the cubs had a chance to sniff it over and put two and two together when Moonshadow started to limp on her burning foot.

She had been bitten by scorpions before, so her body did not react excessively to the poison. Walking was not difficult and the family was several miles closer to home by the time the evening star came out in the gray-purple sky of dusk. Again the keen noses of the coyotes picked up a new smell on the chill night breeze that they were always checking. This time the smell made them quicken their pace and turn up toward a steep incline that they had just skirted. The odor led them to a half-eaten mule deer, an old tooth-worn buck that had wandered into the hunting range of one of the few remaining cougars in that region. The cougar had partly covered the carcass with earth and brush, perhaps to let others know that it was his and that he would be back.

Many cougars had been chased and cornered by hounds and shot when they became outlaws after killing ranch stock. Some men hunted the "lions" for sport. The cougar was one of a dying race. It sought seclusion far away from man in the ravines and gullies of the dry uplands. Because food was scarce, and because of its large body, it had to catch plenty of food each day so as not to starve, and it had a large hunting range. At one time there were plenty of deer for cougars, but the deer became scarce after they had damaged much of their

45

natural grazing land because of their numbers. They were too numerous because cougars (and in other regions, wolves), who kept the deer population down, had been almost exterminated by man. With no natural check, the deer population was enormous. They ate everything that was green until there was nothing left; then they starved to death by the thousands.

Now cougars had to catch what they could. They would often compete with the coyotes for the same food, and this made it hard for the coyotes. Fortunately cougars only eat fresh meat, so the carrion or dead animals were left to the coyote and other scavengers such as badgers and skunks.

Sundance and the others could smell the cougar's tracks around the kill, and also the strong scent of urine that it had used to mark a nearby bush. They had never met a cougar before, but something in the smell and the fact that there was clearly only one large animal that had killed the deer made them extremely cautious.

Hardly had the feast begun when a great scream-roar of protest and anger came tearing out from an outcrop of rock above them. A moment later a rippling golden body rushed down among the coyotes and the air was filled with roars and yelps as coyotes shot like sparks from the hissing center of cougar rage. Its great paws missed their mark and the nimble coyotes scampered away into the darkness. They could run much faster than he. Cougars, like other wild cats, hide and then rush their prey to close in. The only cat that hunts like a coyote or a wolf is the cheetah, coursing or chasing its prey for some distance. So it was easy for the speedy coyotes to outdistance the cougar, although he chased Celeste for several seconds before he decided that it was hopeless to try and catch her.

With hunger somewhat satisfied after stealing from the cougar's larder, the coyotes slept for a while. Nearing home the next morning, the cubs watched Moonshadow and Longface working together on a slope to catch ground squirrels. These would provide a good meal for the hungry family. But ground squirrels are very difficult to catch. If you are uphill, they run down and escape easily, and if you are at the bottom of the hill, they soon tire you out shooting uphill like rockets and in and out of rocks. Longface loped noisily at the bottom of the slope, alarming the ground squirrels who instinctively ran uphill. At the top of the ridge, almost hidden from view, was Moonshadow, who caught the squirrels easily, as though they were apples dropping out of a tree.

During the heat that afternoon, the family alternately rested and played, reaching home singly or in pairs as the sun was dipping low over the hazy blue mountains in the distance. Sundance came into camp carrying a tortoise shell that he had found, its resident having long since passed away. Longface was gently grooming Moonshadow. Sundance came over to them and dropped the shell in front of Longface, but he did not want to play. Tiredness took over what little high spirits were left, and the cubs were soon asleep. Sundance and Sylvia woke up briefly to nibble cactus thorns out of their paws and Sandboy, stuffed full with ground squirrels, lay on his back with his hot and bruised paws cooling in the night air. It had been a long journey and the cubs had learned much.

6

Man Against Coyote

A few days after the long journey into the upper regions of their territory, Moonshadow and Longface took their family on another long trek, this time across the open scrub plains. They went on many such expeditions, returning to the familiar homesite less and less often. They had hunted the area clean where the cubs had spent their first five months. Now they had the appetites of grown-ups and had to keep on the move, scouring first one hunting area and then another in their range. Longface and Moonshadow would lead the family into a new area and then they would split up to hunt and join up again after a day or more.

On the first trek across the scrubland, the cubs learned another coyote trick from their parents—the badger "partnership." As they approached a large sprawl of prickly-pear cactus, they heard and then saw a grizzly brown lump of fur and muscle wheezing and digging into a mass of thorns and rubble. One of the few surviving badgers in the area was breaking into a pack rat's fortress, which consisted of a pile of dead pieces of cactus, thorny mesquite bush, odd bones, stones and even a tin can and an old work glove, that the rats had packed together to make a yard-wide refuge. Inside of this lived the rats, and the badger was breaking in, the thorns hardly penetrating his thick skin, while his powerful forefeet worked like steam shovels. One of the residents lost its nerve and made a run for it, right between the badger's feet. He made a grab at the rat but missed it and continued digging away. The rat ran blindly right into Longface who had silently crept up right behind the badger. Moonshadow, on the other side of the fortress, soon caught one too. The badger was unaware that he was completely surrounded by seven coyotes and that he was providing them with food. He would not have minded anyway, since he was able to catch his fill, and although he was much smaller than a coyote, he was not afraid of them in the least. When the prairie thrived, a coyote would often follow a badger and wait for him to start digging out prairie dogs. Some say that the coyote would even block up some of the escape holes of the prairie dogs to make the job easier.

50

Some weeks later, Longface spotted three buzzards circling in the far distant haze. As the cubs followed him and Moonshadow, they, too, kept looking up at the birds each time their parents glanced up to check their direction. They were reading an important signpost in the sky and would soon learn that where buzzards fly in circles, there is usually something dead or dying and worth eating on the ground below.

After about two miles, the coyotes were almost beneath the birds, but there was no breeze in their faces to

tell them what lay ahead. Nearby, beneath a bush, lay a dead fox, and a little farther off, a skunk lay dying next to a grizzly brown lump of fur. This was the badger.

Sandboy and Sylvia ran on ahead, drawn to the new thing that they had never smelled before. Their pricked ears and flagging tails indicated that they had found something exciting. Always on the alert for danger and suspicious of anything unusual, Longface and Moonshadow raced forward. Moonshadow snarled and leaped at Sandboy, knocking him head over heels with a powerful slam with her hip. He took this as a challenge since what he had found was food—a dead calf. He got up, shook himself and with hair standing up along his back, tail tucked between his legs and jaws gaping wide, sidled toward his mother, hoping to claim what he thought rightfully belonged to him. But again Moonshadow drove him away, and Longface kept the other cubs away too. Both parents suspected that something was wrong because of the dead animals around the rotting body of the calf. The poison-filled calf had been put there as bait. It was probably dropped from an airplane since there was no telltale human scent around. This was the edge of the grazing range for the ranch cattle in this area. The cubs soon realized that their parents were suspicious of the carcass and they set off.

The dead calf had been injected with 1080, a poison that kills anything that eats even a trace of it. In the war against coyotes, men had used all kinds of poisons that they placed in dead animals which served as bait or lures to attract hungry coyotes. An unwary coyote would eat the bait and die terribly and painfully, wracked by convulsions from strychnine or 1080 (sodium fluoacetate). Sometimes they would hide steel traps with sharp teeth near the bait in the hopes of catching the coyote if he stepped accidentally into it while looking over the carcass. Those coyotes that were not killed were those that were the most suspicious. The careless and the bold ones died. The shy and the wary, who were more skittish at seeing something unusual, lived on and their children tended to be like their parents—more wary and suspicious too. But still, a hungry coyote had to eat and many continued to die from poisoned bait laid out by government agents. A skunk or buzzard that ate a coyote poisoned with 1080 would also die since the poison stayed active for a long time. Some government agents used grain soaked in 1080 to kill rodents on farms. Cats, dogs, skunks, eagles and coyotes that ate any of these rodents would also die.

In the early days of the settlers, it was easy to catch a coyote just by placing a piece of meat between the open jaws of a steel trap. Curiosity killed many coyotes too. A rag or bush soaked with some unusual or exciting smell like the odor of a strange coyote would attract an unsuspecting animal. It would soon be caught in one of the hidden traps that encircled the smelly lure. An even more horrible weapon was the "coyote getter." This was a gun loaded with cyanide, a deadly poison, that went off in the coyote's face as soon as it smelled and touched the end of the lure, which was a bulb smeared with some fascinating smelly material. Today the offspring of coyotes who lived through these dangers avoid almost anything unusual in their territory and are rarely caught with traps.

A few of these wily coyotes can be caught because of their fixed habits. Once a coyote has jumped over a fence or rock which is on its trail, it will put its feet in the same place every time. A trap hidden in the right spot on the coyote's trail can catch it. If a den is found, one or more traps will be hidden near the entrance and the unwary parent caught. It is terrible to think of helpless young cubs crying for their mother and then slowly starving to death while she is held fast in a trap two feet away. Some coyotes have bitten off the trapped foot to free themselves.

Most of the night Sundance and his family kept on the move. By dawn they were well into the grazing area of the range cattle. The cubs were fascinated by the scent and droppings of these large, slow animals. Under the sun-dried droppings they found succulent grubs and insects, and the stools passed by calves, which contained much partially-digested milk, were both tasty and nutritious when found fresh.

Coyotes waste nothing and examine everything. When some ranchers see a coyote following closely behind a cow and calf, they shoot to kill, thinking the coyote is out to kill the calf. More often, the innocent coyote is simply after what the calf leaves behind. But sometimes coyotes, who are always crazy for play and are full of tricks of all kinds, will grab a calf by the tail and play tug-of-war. They will do this with each other, but when it hurts, the coyote at the front protests and the other lets go. When it hurts a calf or a steer, it just kicks and runs. More calves have lost their tails than coyotes have gotten black eyes from this game on the scrubland prairie.

Sundance and his family scoured the grazing land of the cattle that lay at the edge of their hunting range. The cubs soon lost their fear of the big, slow, brown and white beasts that seemed constantly to be eating and burping as they ruminated or chewed their cud. Some of the older cattle ignored the coyotes, knowing that they would do them no harm, although some younger steers were skittish.

One day while Sundance was napping under a thorn bush, exhausted from chasing gophers, he woke up with a start when he felt hot, sweet breath in his face. He found himself surrounded by three curious steers, the boldest of which was actually sniffing him. They backed off a little when he woke up and looked at them, but when Sundance continued to lie there, they edged slowly forward again. Sundance was not too sure what they would do next, so he stood up, and immediately the animals stopped advancing. They just stood there, staring. His move next. It looked like a game, and he readied

to run at them. The biggest steer lowered his head, snorted and stamped his foot and then wheeled around and ran off, suddenly stopping when the other two caught up with him. Then all three turned to face Sundance again. He stalked and rushed at them and at the last moment they turned and ran off a short distance and then again stopped and waited for him. They played like this for about half an hour, until Sundance grew bored and went off into the scrubland where he met up with Sylvia and Celeste in search of anything edible in the parched and barren land.

Grasshoppers were plentiful but were only a snack, like potato chips, and no one can live off such a diet for long! Gophers and deer mice were to be found and rabbits were occasionally caught especially when the coyotes worked in pairs—one flushing out the prey and the other chasing it down. Sometimes Sundance would work in a rain-cut gully, driving rabbits and other small prey out of hiding to run down the gully toward Celeste or Sylvia who were ready to ambush them.

One gray, cloudy morning the family heard the screaming of jackrabbits in the distance. It sounded as though dozens of rabbits were in distress. The noise drew the coyotes like a magnet. The sound of a rabbit in trouble will attract all kinds of animals—bobcats, red and gray foxes and coyotes—who think they might get an easy meal. Suddenly they heard the sound of shotguns in the distance. Longface and Moonshadow knew that this sound meant man and they were afraid. It was this fear of men and their natural shyness of the unfamiliar that helped them survive. The cubs sensed the fear in their parents that the sound of guns brought on, but strong-headed Sandboy and Sylvia took off together in the direction of the sounds. Moonshadow uttered a warning bark but the two cubs ignored her. The screaming of rabbits combined with hunger did something to their minds, drawing them closer.

An annual hunt was going on. Each year at this time, ranchers and sportsmen from miles around came with whistles that they blew to call up coyotes and other varmints. The noise their whistles made was like the scream of a rabbit in pain, and with it they could attract all kinds of predators close enough to shoot. Many young and unwary foxes and coyotes were killed in this way, and the man who killed the most over the weekend would be given a prize. In the old days, a hunter might get at least three or four bobcats, half a dozen coyotes and as many foxes in his weekend of fun.

Ignoring Moonshadow's warning, Sandboy and Sylvia raced toward the hunters who were waiting for them, concealed behind hides made of piled sage and mesquite bush. The high, piercing scream of a rabbit, coming from under a large pile of brush, drew the cubs closer and closer. Suddenly shots rang out. Sandboy wheeled to one side and kept running. A hunter cursed at missing him, but his partner had shot Sylvia through the chest.

She ran forward a short way and felt the ground hit her as her legs turned into putty. She rolled over and tried desperately to get up, but her chest was filling with blood. She was drowning in her own blood, wheezing and coughing as it flowed and bubbled out of her mouth. Before she died, the hunter had cut off her tail to record another kill. Then her eyes closed for the last time.

Meanwhile, Sandboy, although he had kept running, had been hit in the stomach. He continued to run for about a mile, until the pain in his side forced him to rest and find shelter. He lay panting under a mesquite bush, licking the hole in his side and straining as the pain increased each time he turned to tend his wound. As night fell, he lay still, feeling less pain now because his body was racked with fever and thirst.

The next morning a cloud of dust came roaring and bouncing over the scrubland. It was a pickup truck loaded with tracker dogs and men who had come to clean up the area. They would find any dying animal that the hunters had not killed by following its scent or bloody trail and shoot it or let their dogs finish it off. In some ways this was a kindness to the injured wild animals that would never get well again. Only too often coyotes and other creatures are injured and left to die slowly and miserably.

After a while they found Sandboy's bloody trail that led them to his hiding place. He heard them coming and summoning all his strength tried to escape, but he could no longer use his hind legs. He dragged himself deeper under the bush and turned to face the oncoming dogs, opening his jaws wide in defense. Bravely he kept the dogs off until the men arrived. The driver of the truck got a rope to drag Sandboy out into the open so he could watch the dogs finish him off. But his companion, who admired the plucky coyote's courage, pushed his companion to one side and mercifully shot Sandboy through the head.

A few days later, Sundance and the others came across the remains of Sandboy and Sylvia. Their bodies had been eaten by the scavengers of the scrubland— buzzards, skunks and flesh-eating insects of many kinds. Nothing is ever wasted in this harsh land.

Sundance sniffed what was left of Sylvia and whined softly, pawing at her back as though to make her get up. Although there was little left of her, he recognized her scent. He also picked up the strange scent of dogs and men, and the hair along his back stood up in alarm. He would never forget these smells, and the sound of guns and the too-strong-to-be-true scream of the rabbit calls still rang in his ears.

7

Run for Your Life

The morning after a severe thunderstorm swept across the scrubland and filled and burst the gullies and arroyos. Soon after, the coyotes saw buzzards in the sky. They took off in their direction, and sure enough, beneath the birds lay their dinner. It was a young steer that had been struck and killed by lightning. More birds gathered in the sky, afraid to come down until the coyotes had finished their feast.

At first the coyotes were extremely cautious because the carcass could have been poisoned. Longface and

Moonshadow carefully sniffed everything and then began to eat, starting first on the dead animal's belly where the skin was thinnest and easier to tear open. They ate well and their evening chorus was long and sweet.

Perhaps it was their singing or the buzzards in the sky that brought another family of coyotes to feed off the steer the next day. Even though there was plenty for all, still the wariness of coyotes toward strangers came out. Longface growled and Moonshadow bristled all over.

Sundance and Celeste were confused. They were excited by the oncoming strangers and at the same time wary, especially in view of their parents' reactions. Sundance growled and wagged his tail, while Celeste kept jumping up and down, coyly looking away each time she jumped up. Suddenly Moonshadow trotted forward, with tail low and wagging and lips pulled back in a friendly grin. She greeted the leading coyote, who was her brother, Raincloud. He accepted her hugs and kisses graciously, standing stiffly with head high and ears up, and remained still for a long time while she sniffed him all over. Then he sprang to life and jumped over and around her in the wildest of greetings. Moonshadow yelped and giggled and rolled over onto her side, and then Raincloud sniffed her all over in turn.

While he was doing this, his mate, Grayeyes, rushed over and punched Moonshadow in the back with open jaws. Moonshadow leaped up and snarled at Grayeyes, who had given her no more than a coyote kick in the pants to let her know who was who. Raincloud whined, trotted over to his wife and licked her on the side of the face. Immediately she snarled at Moonshadow, as though to get Raincloud to join her in an attack on Moonshadow. Raincloud ignored this and slowly walked back to Moonshadow and kissed her. The females then kept their distance, and neither of them challenged nor fought the other again.

Longface, who had been carefully observing all of this, slowly walked toward the three, standing by the steer's carcass. Grayeyes lowered her head, arched her back, and bristling all over, opened her jaws wide as he

approached. She rushed at him and gave him the lightest nip on the shoulder. He ignored her, and she pushed and nipped at him again. Then he turned and growled at her and she immediately rolled over. He sniffed her, and then stood still when she sheepishly got up and sniffed him all over. He looked at Raincloud and walked over to a nearby bush. Hardly taking his eyes off the other male for one moment, he urinated on the bush and then vigorously scraped the earth afterwards. He walked over and stood by Moonshadow and watched Raincloud walk over to the same bush and mark it himself.

With these ritual preliminaries over, the adults began to eat, leaving the cubs to figure things out for themselves. There were three cubs in Raincloud's family, one a girl named Cocoa, who was an unusual chocolate-brown; Lofty, a tall spindle-legged boy; and Starfire, a girl cub with wild eyes and beautiful, almost silvery fur. Whenever any of the cubs approached the adults, they were driven off with snaps and snarls, even by their own parents. The parents themselves tended to avoid or ignore each other as they feasted, although Longface kept giving Moonshadow reassuring licks and nose pushes and Raincloud kept himself between Grayeyes and his sister, Moonshadow.

The cubs, after a few minutes of confused greeting, licking, giggling, nipping, yelping, rolling-over, growling, bristling, standing over and snapping, had things worked out too. How they did it was amazing, since most of the time all six of them were just one great ball of fur and dust, and no one was hurt in the melee. Sundance was dominant over Lofty, Starfire lorded it over Cocoa, and Droopy simply ignored Celeste (of whom she was a little unsure, if not afraid). Lofty and Celeste were friendly toward each other, but something had happened to Starfire. Whenever Sundance came near, she would roll over and scream and then rush at him if he dared walk away, and nip him repeatedly in the shoulder. At first Sundance was confused and made ready to fight, but as soon as he growled, she would roll over at his feet. This was coyote love, and Starfire had clearly fallen for Sundance. When he eventually started to approach her sideways, with the hair on his back fluffed up, tail stuck stiffly out and head high—a proud, assertive display—it was clear that her attention had affected him.

The families split up and went their separate ways, scurrying over the hot flatlands when they heard the distant sound of horses' hooves. Ranchers had seen the buzzards and had decided to check things out after the storm. It could be a calf stuck in a muddy gully or a cow having difficulty giving birth. When they found the dead steer and the signs of several coyotes around the well-eaten carcass, they mistakenly reckoned that the coyotes had killed the steer. They returned later and buried several traps around the carcass, since their supply of poison had been used up. With these traps they hoped to catch at least one of the innocent animals that they had outlawed, if it returned to feed again.

At the ranch they got together and arranged a hunt for the next day. With their buddies, hounds and guns they would make a day of it, scouring the scrubland and killing anything smaller than a calf that moved.

The following day they drove out to the dead steer. The traps that the two ranchers had hidden had caught nothing. One of their buddies jumped off the truck to look at the steer's teeth to figure out how old it was. He didn't know that traps had been planted around it. The ranchers gave a shout, but too late. *Clunk*, a trap snapped and a ranch hand was caught. The teeth of the trap cut through his dry, cracked boot as though it were cardboard and sunk deep into his ankle. He yelled in surprise and pain and cursed as his friends pried the trap off his leg. To admit that it hurt much would have been a sign of weakness, so although in much pain, he insisted on going on with the hunt. The more his ankle hurt, the more he wanted to kill coyotes. He was the driver, and it would be a wild ride for the others, since it was his right ankle that was hurt and he needed this to operate the foot brake on the truck. Because it was his truck and his idea in the first place to have fun getting coyotes, he had his own way on this day.

One of the men climbed on top of the pickup and scanned the scrubland with a pair of powerful binoculars. He looked thoroughly, especially in the shadows under the bushes and clumps of bunch grass for telltale movements or coyotelike forms. He saw nothing and was just about to get down from the truck when he noticed a movement in a thick clump of bunch grass. He had caught Sundance snapping at a blowfly. Quickly the dogs and men piled into the truck and drove right at Sundance. As soon as he ran from cover, the men started to shoot, but with the truck bouncing on the rough ground and Sundance dodging and swerving between the bushes, they kept missing. The driver shifted gears and pressed harder in pursuit of Sundance to tire him out. Then they would release the dogs to finish him off.

Sundance was terrified, but he did not lose his head in a wild fast run to escape. He kept up a steady pace, zigzagging and making a wide circle that was difficult for the truck to follow.

Suddenly the truck ground to a halt, the front wheels skidding and locking as the vehicle nose-dived into a deep, narrow gully that the driver did not see in his excitement. His injured right leg slowed down his reactions, and behind him the dogs and riders in the back went sprawling in a heap of yelps and curses. The driver cracked the truck into reverse, and with a roar, the old pickup slowly pulled out. Since they could not cross the gully in pursuit, they set the dogs after Sundance. These were fast dogs, two of them greyhounds, and the other three part greyhound and part bloodhound. The men watched and whooped as they saw their dogs rapidly closing in on Sundance. But suddenly Sundance took off as though he had wings. Given a fair start he could have outrun any of them, but he was tiring fast now and was not able to keep up his speed for long.

The men lost sight of the chase and did not see Longface come out of hiding and lope toward the dogs, making himself obvious and moving slowly as though he would be easy for them to catch. He was using himself as a decoy to draw the dogs away from Sundance. He was fresh and could easily outrun them and give Sundance the chance to escape. He had done this before when Moonshadow was in a similar predicament, and his mother had done it for him when he was not much older than Sundance.

The lead dog, a tiger-striped and much scarred hound, took off after Longface, but Sundance was not safe yet.

One of the more experienced hounds was wise to what was happening, and he and a bitch dog continued to pursue Sundance.

By now Sundance was exhausted, his mouth wide

open, gasping for breath, and his eyes wide with fear. Many a coyote in this state would keep on, running blindly until he felt the hounds' jaws close on his rump or neck and the chase would soon be over. But Sundance did not panic. Right in his path lay a deep, rain-washed and sun-split gully. He jumped down and ran along it, searching for a refuge in which he could hide or at least protect himself. He could hear the panting of the hounds and the pad of their racing feet on the ground close behind him, and he almost panicked and missed what he was looking for. Just before the dogs leaped at him, he spotted a hole in the side of the gully. It was just deep enough to cover him up to the shoulders. A badger had been along digging for gophers and had unwittingly helped save Sundance's life.

He leaped into the hole and as the first dog bit him in the rump, he twisted around and faced his two opponents. A coyote's skin is loose, like a bag, and Sundance was able to twist around inside it and bite back at the dog that was holding onto him. Instantly, the dog let go, bleeding from a saberlike wound that Sundance's razor teeth had inflicted across his face. The second dog lunged into the hole but was also driven away by courageous Sundance. With his back protected in the hole, he could defend himself easily against the two dogs, at least for a while. The dogs retreated, and then, one by one, started to lunge at Sundance, one approaching from one side hoping to draw him out, while the other would strike from the other side. The first time they tried this, they almost succeeded. The large male hound tore Sundance's ear, but missed getting a firm hold on his neck. After this near miss, Sundance was not fooled again. Their last resort was to sit and wait by the hole, in the hopes that fear or thirst would eventually drive Sundance out of his refuge. Sundance held fast, but almost bolted when he heard a man coming and calling for his dogs. The dogs started to bark excitedly and resume their attacks on Sundance. It was the same man who had mercifully shot Sandboy instead of letting his companion set his dogs onto the dying coyote.

He gruffly called off his dogs and raised his gun to fire. He could not miss. If Sundance ran from the hole at the last second, the dogs would get him anyway. He took careful aim, getting his sights in line with a point right between Sundance's eyes. He had never looked a coyote in the eye, but he did just this before he pulled the trigger. Sundance was looking him straight in the face, his expression showing both fear and a curious kind of waiting. The man's finger was automatically closing on the trigger, but it suddenly froze. Sundance's eyes reminded him of how his own young son sometimes looked at him. That look of fear when his son had done something wrong, and that curious look as he waited for an answer or for forgiveness. The sights of the barrel wavered and the gun grew heavy until his arms began to shake uncontrollably.

The dogs looked at their master and then, one by one, walked over to him, with sheepish expressions on their faces and tails wagging but low and soft. The man was on his knees now, with his head buried in his hands. The dogs licked his face, even though he tried weakly to push them away.

71

Then, with a sigh, he sat down right in front of Sundance and slowly rolled a cigarette to settle his nerves so that he could think for a while. His mind was buzzing, trying to put together what had happened. The more he analyzed, the less progress he made. What had caused him not to shoot Sundance? He knew that the other dogs had flushed out another coyote and had gone after it, but perhaps as his father once told him as a boy, it could have been a decoy coyote that had put its life on the line to save its companion.

Gradually he began to relax his mind and body. Sundance brought him back to the here and now. An absentmindedly-flipped cigarette butt lay smoldering in front of Sundance and made him sneeze. The man watched. Cautiously, Sundance put out a paw and touched the curious, smoking object. Then he looked at the man and drew back into the hole, to wait, and to watch also.

Then the man began to take in the whole scene; the dry scrubland that his father remembered as prairie, his dogs, cousins of the coyote, that would even play and mate with coyotes when left alone. Instead, he had trained them to kill their coyote relatives. Underneath he knew that coyotes did more good than harm and that only the odd renegade would ever kill a calf. But he went along with the others in poisoning and shooting them. He didn't want to feel left out or, worse, to be branded as a softie.

From now on though, he would kill no more coyotes. If they left him alone, he would do the same. With no more ado, he spat in the dust, put the safety catch on his gun, leashed his dogs and strode back across the plains to join his companions.

Sundance watched them until they were out of sight and then he stealthily crawled out of his life-saving badger hole. He paused briefly to sniff the cigarette butt around where the man had been sitting. Then he rolled on the butt, the smell of tobacco exploding into his nose as he rubbed it into his neck and shoulders. As a final act, gesture, or whatever, he urinated on the shredded paper. On the edge of the gully he stood up, raised his head to the pale moon, gave his *ye-yee-yee-yeeeii* call, and was answered by four other voices scattered across the plain. He moved toward one of them, and within half an hour the family was united again. That night they sang together for a long time, and the Indian dogs on a distant reservation answered them with barks and howls. Although life was hard, and often cruel, love, friendship and belonging were rewards enough.

8

Sundance and Laughing Dog

Two months later though, the family began to break up. The breeding season was beginning and Moonshadow and Longface were spending more and more time together and kept driving the cubs away. They would perhaps have another litter of cubs in the spring, and to have their grown-up children around at the same time would have meant a shortage of food. There was simply not enough to go around for a large family of coyotes.

Although coyote families break up when the cubs are

about ten months of age, to make room for more cubs, the family ties are still strong between parents and grown-up cubs. It is not so easy for young coyotes, since it is usually difficult for them to find an unoccupied territory for themselves.

Sundance and Droopy were left to go their separate ways, to seek a place many miles from their parents' range. As often happens, one of the cubs stayed with the parents and moved back with them to the old den site in the arroyo. This was Celeste. She would act as nurse-maid and babysitter when Moonshadow had her next litter.

Sundance settled down to work an area that over-lapped the far edge of his parents' territory and the haz-ardous ranch land where men made room for little else except their cattle. At the north end of his range was an Indian reservation, consisting of some poor grazing land and a village of adobe mud huts, chickens, sheep and dogs. The Indians, who worked for the ranchers some-times, had a little land themselves that they irrigated and cultivated with great care and pride. These Indians were once lords of the prairie, living in harmony with nature. But now they had no prairie, only ghostly memories of their past glory and a little pride and tradition that held them together as a community.

Very early in the morning, just before the roosters began to crow, Sundance would slink around the Indian reservation, jump over a low stone wall and hunt around for goodies in the village dump. He liked to go there, even though there was usually little garbage worth eating because the Indians wasted very little and the village

75

dogs ate whatever there was. Sometimes he would find an old boot, a shredded pancho or a worn-out piece of leather harness. The taste and smells of these things excited him—horse, man, spice, sweat, dust, filled him with fear and also gave him a sense of power. Power, because he could drag or carry these finds off into the scrubland and play with them to his heart's content. Also at that time of the morning, there were rats and mice on the dump for Sundance to catch.

One morning at the dump he had a strange visitor, the likes of whom he had never seen before. It had a cylindrical metal head which it would clank and swing on the ground, and a black and white body that stuck out behind.

In its frenzy to get its stuck head out of a tin can, a skunk blundered blindly into things and made quite a noise. Sundance leaped backward each time the tin can struck something solid and then edged forward cautiously when the poor skunk paused for breath.

The noise woke up a very light sleeper who lived in the adobe hut that was nearest to the dump. Laughing Dog, an Indian boy who was eleven years old that very day, poked his head out of the square, open window that looked out toward the dump. He watched what was going on, fascinated by the antics of the skunk and by the curiosity of Sundance. Slipping on his sandals and pancho, he crept out into the twilight, along a low wall that gave him good cover, until he was only a few yards away from the dump. There, he had a closer look. He saw that the skunk with the metal head was getting nowhere trying to free itself.

The sight of Sundance filled him with awe. He had

always wanted a coyote ever since his cousin had a coyote cub. They dug it out of a den on hearing its cries after a rancher had shot its mother out on the plains. Unfortunately, his cousin's cub died from distemper that it caught from one of the village dogs.

It was getting light now, and the first of the village dogs began to bark. Sundance pricked his ears, and still wary of dogs, ran off into the scrubland, leaving Laughing Dog and the skunk, trapped by its own greed and curiosity in the tin can. Laughing Dog quietly approached the skunk, grabbed the tin can and held it up. This was all that the skunk needed to break free, and a moment later Laughing Dog was alone on the dump. He hurried back home for breakfast, bursting to tell his parents and little sister all that he had seen. He also decided that from then on he would wake up early every morning and look out for Sundance again. He spent that day wondering how he could become friends with the coyote, but there seemed no way that he could ever get close to that swift, wild animal of the plains.

Laughing Dog had kept all kinds of pets that he caught or found injured in the desert—lizards, a gila woodpecker, a burrowing owl, lots of baby rabbits and a baby badger, which soon dug its way out of the orange crate that he kept it in and escaped. Once he even had a little kit fox that his mother helped him raise, since its eyes weren't even open when it was found. This little fox used to play with his two house cats, but one day a pack of village dogs broke into the backyard and killed it. His parents, like the rest of the Indians on the reservation loved, respected and understood the wild creatures that lived around them.

77

Although his parents were poor and had little food to spare, they encouraged Laughing Dog's interest in animals and gave him whatever advice or food he needed to look after his pets. His mother warned him about rabid animals and instructed him how to recognize a sick skunk, fox or coyote that might seem friendly and come right up to him. But a rabid animal bites in a blind fury and in so doing, gives the disease to any person, or other animal that it bites.

She also taught him how to handle his pets gently, but firmly, and how to nurse them, feed them and even mend broken legs and wings. His father showed him how to hunt and trap, but Laughing Dog did not like to do this. This made him feel unhappy, because he did want to please his father and do the grown-up, manly things that he did. But he did like to go out with his father and learn to recognize the tracks and sounds of the animals, and where and when they might be found.

He spent many hours listening to his father's stories, at bedtime and around the fire when they camped out in the scrubland—stories about how all the animals in the desert get along with each other and how each one is important and neither better nor worse than another. Each one has its place, and the Indian too. Although man was lord over the other animals because of his greater intelligence, this did not mean that they were his to destroy or to do whatever he wished to, as many of the ranchers had done.

Laughing Dog learned what the prairies used to be like, full of buffalo, antelope, prairie dogs and lush, rolling grass. His father also told him many Indian legends, like the one of the two bull buffaloes who fought in the clouds and made thunder. There was a coyote who made the sun and so brought life to earth. Other coyotes had whispered about the future into the ears of those they chose to speak to while they lay sleeping under the stars, and gave great wisdom to them. Laughing Dog learned that his great-grandfather, sleeping out in the prairie during a hunting trip, heard a coyote speak to him in his dreams. When he woke up, he was a very different man and he eventually became chief. He said that a coyote had taken him on a long dream journey and had shown him the beginning and the end of the world and had revealed to him the secret of life which he could tell to no man. Perhaps what the rancher felt that stopped him from shooting Sundance was something close to this experience, but his mind was not open enough to see as much as Laughing Dog's great-grandfather.

At first Laughing Dog was thought by his playmates to be a softie, because he didn't like to kill animals. He told his friends that their lives were different now. They had their own corn and sheep and cattle and other food supplies from the trading post, and so had no need or right to keep on hunting and killing wild animals for food. He told them the wild animals had a difficult enough time with all the domestic livestock eating every- thing up. They teased him less and less and began to listen to what he said. Respect grew for his ability to heal sick and injured animals. He even had a way with lame horses, and sick calves and lambs. He once tamed a wild horse by whispering to it in a soft voice and stroking it gently when everyone else except his father had given up. His father knew now that one day his son would take his place as chief.

79

9

Starfire and Freedom

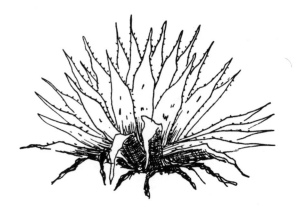

Sundance got used to seeing Laughing Dog on those early morning meetings. Day by day Laughing Dog was able to get closer and closer to Sundance as he began to lose his fear of the boy. Laughing Dog was patient and did not rush things, but one day when he threw something at Sundance, the suspicious coyote ran off. He thought Laughing Dog was threatening him. Only later, when he returned, did he discover that it was food and not a rock that Laughing Dog had thrown at him. Shortly after, the Indian boy could stand waiting for Sundance to come and the coyote would approach within a couple of yards to be fed. Often, Sundance would be there waiting before Laughing Dog arrived. The boy always spoke in a soft, coaxing voice, but one morning he called, *"Yei-yei-yeee,"* just before he threw him the food. He was training Sundance to come, and from then on he would give the call whenever he got to the dump before Sundance.

Three morning later Sundance wagged his tail for the first time as a greeting to Laughing Dog. Sundance recognized and accepted him as a friend now, although he would not let the boy get close enough to touch him.

Suddenly Sundance pricked his ears, looked toward the west and then ran off at top speed, leaving behind the food that Laughing Dog had just thrown to him. Soon Laughing Dog discovered what had so alarmed his fleet-footed friend. A ranch hand was bouncing toward the reservation in a rusty, old jeep that sent up a plume of dust into the pale blue sunrise sky. He spotted Laughing Dog's silhouette on the skyline and drove up to him. The jeep was crammed with camping gear, guns, ammunition and traps; hacked-up pieces of steer were roped onto the back—poisoned bait. The ranch hand pushed his hat back, and squinting against the glare of the rising sun, looked up at Laughing Dog on top of the mound and asked him if he had seen any coyotes. Laughing Dog, who always told the truth, said that he had seen coyotes many, many times. "How about today?" asked the man. "What about today?" asked Laughing Dog. "Darn it," said the ranchhand. "Have you seen any coyotes round here right now?" "No, not right now," said Laughing Dog, which was the truth. Then he ran off saying he had to go and get his breakfast. He wondered if the man had seen him feeding Sundance and if he would try to trap or poison any wild animals near the reservation. He would tell his parents about the man. His father would know what to do.

The man jumped out of the jeep and checked the ropes that held the poisoned meat secure to the vehicle. He limped as he walked. It was the same man who had injured his foot in the trap and who had wanted to set the dogs onto Sandboy. He was having a few days vacation, and the best fun for him was going out after coyotes. It was a one-man war—him against the coyote nation. And he didn't like Indians either, simply because he never bothered to try to understand them or their ways.

Sitting next to him was his best friend, a part greyhound, part bloodhound coyote killer. The dog had a keen nose for tracking coyotes and was fast and strong. Its master had trained it to be a killer. Ropes secure, he limped back on a permanently twisted ankle, and jumped into the seat, spitting a wad of spent chewing tobacco onto the ground.

He needed fresh water and went to fill his cans from the well in the village. The children were curious about his traps and guns, but they kept away when he cursed and kicked at a couple of village dogs that were sniffing at the poisoned meat tied to the jeep. Then the dogs started to bark at him and his dog because they were both strangers. More dogs came and the noise sounded as if there were a war on.

Laughing Dog's father walked up to the man, greeted him, and asked him what he wanted. He was welcome to the water from the well. Then he reminded the ranch hand that no hunting or trapping was allowed on their reservation, but yes, since he was a neighbor he could camp out on the reservation. Laughing Dog's father didn't want the man anywhere near the reservation, but because he was a neighbor, he felt he couldn't refuse him.

The man drove off, with a trail of dogs and children chasing him noisily out of the village. He set up camp behind a range of hills about two miles from the village. He was going to get as many coyotes as he could over the next four days and he would hunt them on the reservation, rules or no rules. His point was that coyotes came off the reservation, killed his stock on the range and then ran back to their dens and the safety of the reservation. The few coyotes that lived on the reservation did sometimes kill a sheep, lamb or calf owned by the Indians, but this happened seldom. The Indians accepted these losses as part of life, and they also accepted the coyote as more friend or ally than enemy because he kept down rodents and other unwanted pests that took the food meant for their livestock.

That day the ranch hand and his dog sleuthed around for signs of coyotes—trails, scent posts, droppings—and found plenty. He called them up that night by howling like a coyote, and he could do it very well. All around him the coyotes began to howl, but he did not know what they were saying to each other.

Laughing Dog also heard the coyotes singing that night and felt there was something different in the way they howled. He prayed that Sundance would be safe and that the ranch hand would respect the law not to kill any wild animals on the reservation.

There was a clear full moon that night, making it easy for the man and his hound to find coyote trails and put down traps and poison bait. His dog picked up one of Sundance's trails. It was the one that Sundance took to the dump every morning. He saw the paw prints in the ground where Sundance landed after jumping over the stone wall on his way to meet Laughing Dog. Carefully the man dug up the soil in the exact spot where Sundance would land and neatly buried a steel trap there. His hatred for coyotes made it more important for him to kill them than to obey the law, and he did not care what the Indians said anyway. Before he left, he hurled a piece of poisoned meat onto the dump, knowing that coyotes are scavengers and might well take the bait if it was placed where they would not be suspicious.

Just before sunrise the next morning, Sundance was up and padding along his trail to meet his Indian friend. On the way he found a steer's leg that the man had put down as bait. He was immediately suspicious, since he had never seen anything like it along this trail. As he circled the bait, his sensitive nose detected a familiar smell. Tobacco! The ranch hand had absentmindedly spat on the ground a few yards from the bait. This time Sundance did not roll in it. His hair rose as he remembered all that went on in the badger hole where he fought off two dogs and faced the man with the gun. He sniffed around for some time, picking up the trail of the man and the dog that crisscrossed his trail. He decided to turn back, and that day he did not go to the dump to meet Laughing Dog. The boy thought that Sundance must have been trapped or poisoned, but he resolved to be there the next morning, just in case.

That afternoon, two dogs came staggering into the village, one dying in the main street, after several convulsions. The other rolled around screaming and was humanely shot by one of the Indians. People were screaming "mad dogs"—they thought that the two dogs had rabies. Laughing Dog's father came out to look at them, and before the other dog was put out of its misery he was able to tell that it wasn't rabies. He had seen dogs behave that way and die from 1080. There was no cure for this poison. At once he suspected that they had picked up poison bait put down by the ranch hand. He was right. They had gone to the dump and eaten the bait

intended for Sundance, who would have certainly eaten
it, thinking that his friend, Laughing Boy, had put it
there.

Next morning, Laughing Boy was waiting for Sundance. His eyes lit up when he saw the coyote jump over
the wall but he screamed when he saw what happened
when Sundance landed. He landed right where he
always did, but this time the open trap was waiting for
him. Sundance yelped with pain, leaped time after time
into the air, twisting and pulling, but the anchor hook
on the trap held firm. The steel jaws of the trap had
snapped tight and the teeth were fixed deep into the
tendons and bone of his foot. In pain and fear, Sundance
fought for freedom, but the more he pulled, the more the
teeth dug into his paw. He bit at the trap and snapped at

a nearby bush in desperation. There was no way out. He then lay still, panting, blood gushing from his paw and from his mouth where he had bitten his tongue in trying to escape.

He heard footsteps, the heavy footsteps of a man, and he lay still, playing dead and not even looking. Suddenly he heard a familiar voice; it was Laughing Dog and the man was his father whom he had awakened to come and help.

His father had known about his son's coyote friend for a long time, because food was always disappearing from the storeroom and he had heard Laughing Dog get up early one morning and had watched him through the window. What he saw then made him feel good. When he was a boy, he, too, once had a coyote friend.

Sundance lay still, with his eyes fixed on Laughing Dog. The boy's father stood back a way after he had examined the poor animal's foot, so as not to scare the coyote.

He instructed his son in a quiet voice on what to do. He told Laughing Dog that his coyote would probably lose the foot, but if they let him free he would probably survive, since many a coyote has been found in the wild doing well on three legs. But Laughing Dog, through his tears, said: "No, Father. I want to take him home and try to save his foot. Anyway, my sister Morning Light will help, and we can't let the ranch man get him after this."

Perhaps for this reason alone, Laughing Dog's father agreed to take Sundance back to the village. He pulled his belt off and muzzled the coyote, so that he would not bite them out of fear or pain when they handled his injured foot. Laughing Dog used his belt as a leash, just in case Sundance tried to run off with the muzzle on. He then touched Sundance for the first time. He felt the soft fur, speckled with dust, saliva and blood flecks and sensed the energy and strength beneath it. Sundance looked away and put his ears back and tried to roll over to show his submission and acceptance of Laughing Dog. Suddenly Laughing Dog had to sit on him and use all his strength to hold the poor animal down as his father pried open the trap. They left the trap where it was.

The boy carried Sundance home. With nylon fishing line, they stitched up the torn skin as best they could, after washing the terrible wound with cool boiled water and antiseptic. Laughing Dog's father thought that some of the smaller bones in the foot were broken, but that they should heal without needing a splint. They chained Sundance up in the quiet backyard, and as a den they gave him a packing crate, in which to hide and feel safe. Laughing Dog put out food and water after his father had taken off the muzzle, but Sundance lay shaking in the back of the crate, with his head pressed into the far corner out of fear and shock.

Wisely, they left him alone to settle down. Laughing Dog's sister was busy making up more food for Sundance while his father was having a conference with the elders about what to do with the ranch hand who was now on their land illegally, since he had trapped and killed animals. His father took them to where Sundance had been caught and showed them the trap lying there. One of the elders went to fetch the sheriff and they presented the evidence to him. The village community was angry, since they had many grievances against some of the ranchers and big land-owners. They had been working to have more of the rangeland given back to them, because their reservation was small and hardly sufficient to support them in any way. The sheriff, scared that real trouble might erupt, agreed to go out with two of the elders and get the man to leave the reservation at once.

They found him at his camp with three fresh coyote tails hanging on the spare wheel of the jeep. The sheriff took him to one side, and after a few words, head shakes and nods, the ranch hand packed up and drove off, his brown teeth showing through a sickly grin.

Laughing Dog was angry when he learned from his father that the man had been let go. Surely he should have been punished in some way. "No," said his father. "To punish him would just make him hate coyotes and Indians even more. What we need are stronger laws to protect our reservation and way of life. We cannot afford to waste our energies on small incidents like this. We have been working for years on our legal claim to the rangeland which is common grazing land here and which used to be ours. A fair share must be given back to us to use as we wish. We will not overgraze it, but will give it a new life and restore the prairie. Nothing must get in the way of our goal."

Morning Light came running to them, shouting that Sundance was eating. This is always a good sign, since some wild animals are so terrified when caught that they cannot eat and then die of starvation. Sundance's foot would heal quickly if he ate well. The children took a bowl of milk out to him. He ran back to hide in the crate, but immediately stuck his head out again. They stepped back and he came out and sniffed the milk. Something very new, indeed! Sundance bent low as though to drink

89

and then twisted his head to one side. He was going to roll on it. *Splosh*, the milk spilled all over the place and Sundance hobbled back into the crate and sat at the entrance, looking at the milk and then at Laughing Dog and Morning Light.

He liked and trusted the children, and over the next two weeks his wound healed quickly. He even allowed the children to pet him, and one evening when the children were laughing and playing together in the yard, Sundance began to yip and sing, too.

When Sundance started to put all his weight on the injured foot, they knew that it had healed well and that he was ready to be set free. Laughing Dog wondered if Sundance would run off and never come back—perhaps he would still come and meet him every morning, as before. He really wanted to keep Sundance as a pet and that night he had a long talk with his father. "No, my son," he said, "a wild animal belongs out there with its own kind. You and Morning Light have done well and learned much, but tomorrow you must let him go free."

The next evening, so as to avoid any encounters with the village dogs that might not like Sundance, Laughing Dog took Sundance's chain and led the coyote out to the dump. There he sat, with Sundance leaning against him, the stars in the sky splitting into thousands of pieces as he looked at them through his tears. How could he let Sundance go? He loved him so much. He wanted to keep the coyote but knew that was both selfish and cruel. His father was right. Laughing Dog sniffed and wiped his eyes, but began to cry again when Sundance nuzzled him and whined softly. The beautiful animal sat next to the

Indian boy, waiting and trusting. Laughing Dog knew that Sundance would probably never come to the dump again because of his experience there. He wiped his nose and breathed deeply, a sob catching in his throat. An idea suddenly struck him. Why not run away with Sundance and live out in the wilds with him? They could do it together. Then he remembered he had seen something like that in a movie at the Community Center once. It just wasn't real.

So he set off across the scrubland until he could hardly see the lights of the reservation. Feeling that they were far enough away, he took the chain off the coyote and told him to go away, but stay in the reservation where it would be safe. Sundance whined again and took a few bounding strides into the brush, then he came back to the boy and sat close to him for a while. Laughing Dog sat quite still with his knees up and his chin resting on his hands. He had stopped crying now and was just letting things flow around him and into him as he looked around—the dry earth beneath his sandals, a shining grain of smooth quartz on his toe, a mesquite bean, dry, but ready to explode with life when the rains came, a cricket's song rising and falling on a light breeze that hummed softly through the bushes. He looked up and saw the stars, small, far away, and he imagined that he was a star looking down to earth and seeing Laughing Dog, so small and far away. Then he heard a distant *yip yip yeei yeei yeee*, and Sundance sat up and cocked his ears, then raised his head and answered. He gave Laughing Dog one last, long look and then disappeared in the direction from which the call came.

A little later Laughing Dog was fast asleep, warm in the thick pancho spread around him like a tent. In his dream he saw Sundance meet another coyote out on the range and take her to the hills behind the reservation, where they would be safe and where they could raise their cubs without fear of government trappers and ranchers.

After Sundance had traveled for about a mile, he saw a silver form moving lightly in front of him, a form that suddenly rushed at him and sent him flying. As soon as he got up, there, wriggling at his feet, was Starfire! They reintroduced themselves, played and chased for a while, and eventually Sundance led his mate to the reservation. That would be their territory from now on. They passed the sleeping form of Laughing Dog on their way back. Starfire overcame her shyness when she saw how Sundance trusted him and she sniffed and nibbled at his old pancho, while Sundance nuzzled his cheek as a parting gesture.

Laughing Dog stirred in his sleep and heard a coyote whisper in his ear "Thank you. We are brothers. We are all one. All is one."

He awoke before daybreak. It had started to rain at last. The smell of breakfast greeted him as he walked through the door. The doorway seemed much smaller somehow. His parents smiled, for they knew now that Laughing Dog would be a good chief for his people.

About the Author

Dr. Michael Fox is a noted authority on animal behavior, combining the background of a degree from London's Royal Veterinary School and a PhD in psychology from London University with a profound concern for the well-being and conservation of wildlife.

Dr. Fox is an associate professor of psychology at Washington University. His books about animal behavior, including *Understanding Your Dog, Behavior of Wolves, Dogs and Related Canids, The Wolf,* and *Vixie: The Story of a Little Fox,* are largely based on firsthand observation. Dr. Fox has personally raised coyotes, red, gray, and arctic foxes, timber wolves, jackals, dogs, and cats.

He and his wife, Bonnie, and two children, Wylie and Camilla, make their home in St. Louis, Missouri.

About the Artist

Dee Gates observed and sketched Dr. Fox's own coyotes before beginning her illustrations for *Sundance Coyote*.

She has worked as a horse trainer and for the Jackson County Humane Shelter and was once an assistant to a dog barber!

The artist and her husband, John, live in Wheeling, Illinois, where she enjoys horseback riding, playing the guitar, and drawing.